The Music of SWING Plus One

MW00981176

20 Great Songs To Play With Orchestral Accompaniment CD

Arranged by Tony Esposito
Background instruments performed by Nick Waynelovich for Ja'Duke Prod.

CONTENTS

	PAGE #	TRACK #
AND THE ANGELS SING	3	1
AVENUE "C"	4	2
BEI MIR BIST DU SCHON	6	3
BIG NOISE FROM WINNETKA	8	5
BUGLE CALL RAG	7	4
CHATTANOOGA CHOO CHOO	10	7
COME FLY WITH ME	9	6
DON'T SIT UNDER THE APPLE TREE	12	8
G.I. JIVE	13	9
IT'S NICE TO GO TRAV'LING	14	10
I'VE GOT A GAL IN KALAMAZOO	15	11
JUMPIN' AT THE WOODSIDE	16	12
MOONLIGHT SERENADE	17	13
PENNSYLVANIA 6-5000	18	14
SATURDAY NIGHT (IS THE LONELIEST NIGHT OF THE WEEK)	19	15
SHORTY GEORGE	20	16
STOMPIN' AT THE SAVOY	21	17
STRAIGHTEN UP AND FLY RIGHT	22	18
TAKING A CHANCE ON LOVE	23	20
ZING! WENT THE STRINGS OF MY HEART	24	19

AND THE ANGELS SING

Words by
JOHNNY MERCER

Music by
ZIGGY ELMAN
Arranged by
TONY ESPOSITO

IF9935CD

4　2

AVENUE "C"

Music by
BUCK CLAYTON
Arranged by
TONY ESPOSITO

Bright swing ♩ = 190

3

BEI MIR BIST DU SCHÖN
(Means That You're Grand)

Music by
SHOLOM SECUNDA
Arranged by
TONY ESPOSITO

IF9935CD

BUGLE CALL RAG

Words and Music by
**JACK PETTIS, BILLY MEYERS
and ELMER SCHOEBEL**
*Arranged by
TONY ESPOSITO*

Moderate swing ♩ = 150

IF9935CD

BIG NOISE FROM WINNETKA

Music by
BOB HAGGART and RAY BAUDUC
Arranged by
TONY ESPOSITO

IF9935CD

COME FLY WITH ME

Lyric by
SAMMY CAHN

Music by
JAMES VAN HEUSEN
Arranged by
TONY ESPOSITO

Fast swing ♩ = 170

IF9935CD

CHATTANOOGA CHOO CHOO

Music by
HARRY WARREN
Arranged by
TONY ESPOSITO

Moderate boogie beat ♩ = 120

Chattanooga Choo Choo - 2 - 1
IF9935CD

DON'T SIT UNDER THE APPLE TREE
(With Anyone Else But Me)

Words and Music by
CHARLIE TOBIAS, LEW BROWN
and SAM H. STEPT
Arranged by
TONY ESPOSITO

IF9935CD

G.I. JIVE

Words and Music by
JOHNNY MERCER
Arranged by
TONY ESPOSITO

10

IT'S NICE TO GO TRAV'LING

Lyric by
SAMMY CAHN

Music by
JAMES VAN HEUSEN
Arranged by
TONY ESPOSITO

Fast swing ♩ = 190

IF9935CD

I'VE GOT A GAL IN KALAMAZOO

Music by
HARRY WARREN
Arranged by
TONY ESPOSITO

Moderate swing ♩ = 176

IF9935CD

12

JUMPIN' AT THE WOODSIDE

Music by
COUNT BASIE
Arranged by
TONY ESPOSITO

IF9935CD

MOONLIGHT SERENADE

Music by
GLENN MILLER
Arranged by
TONY ESPOSITO

13

IF9935CD

14

PENNSYLVANIA 6-5000

Music by
JERRY GRAY
Arranged by
TONY ESPOSITO

IF9935CD

SATURDAY NIGHT
(Is The Loneliest Night Of The Week)

Lyric by
SAMMY CAHN

Music by
JULE STYNE
Arranged by
TONY ESPOSITO

15

IF9935CD

16

SHORTY GEORGE

Music by
COUNT BASIE
Arranged by
TONY ESPOSITO

Moderate bounce ♩ = 170

IF9935CD

STOMPIN' AT THE SAVOY

Lyric by
ANDY RAZAF

Music by
BENNY GOODMAN, CHICK WEBB
and EDGAR SAMPSON
Arranged by
TONY ESPOSITO

IF9935CD

STRAIGHTEN UP AND FLY RIGHT

Words and Music by
NAT KING COLE and IRVING MILLS
Arranged by
TONY ESPOSITO

IF9935CD

20 TAKING A CHANCE ON LOVE

Music by
VERNON DUKE
Arranged by
TONY ESPOSITO

IF9935CD

19

ZING! WENT THE STRINGS OF MY HEART

Words and Music by
JAMES F. HANLEY
Arranged by
TONY ESPOSITO